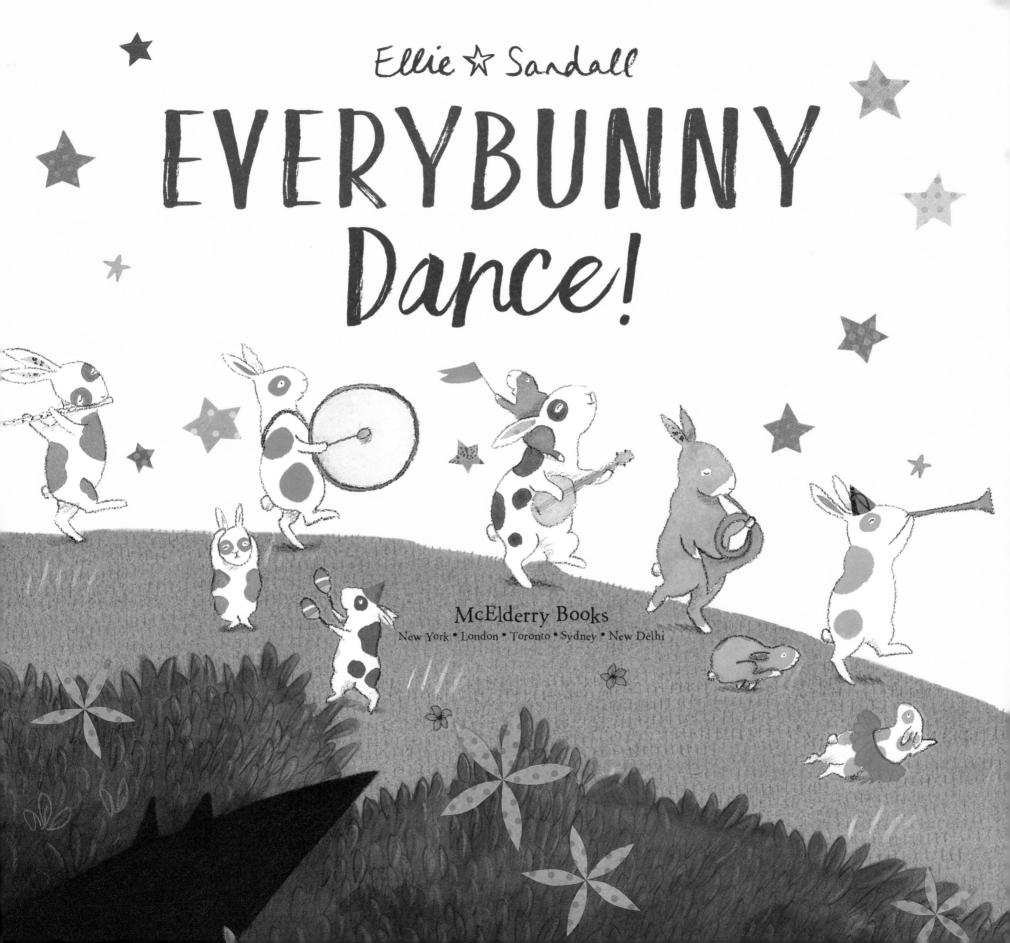

Ellie ☆ Sandall

EVERYBUNNY
Dance!

McElderry Books
New York • London • Toronto • Sydney • New Delhi

Nobody is watching.
Now's the perfect chance.

Ready bunny,

steady bunny,

EVERYBUNNY

DANCE!

And **clap** your paws,

and **twist** and **twirl**,

and **shake** your tail,

and **wiggle** and **whirl**.

And **bang** a drum,

and **play** the flute,

and blow a horn,

a-tooty-toot!

Fa-la-la-la, tra-la-la-lee,

doo-dooby-doo, fiddle-de...

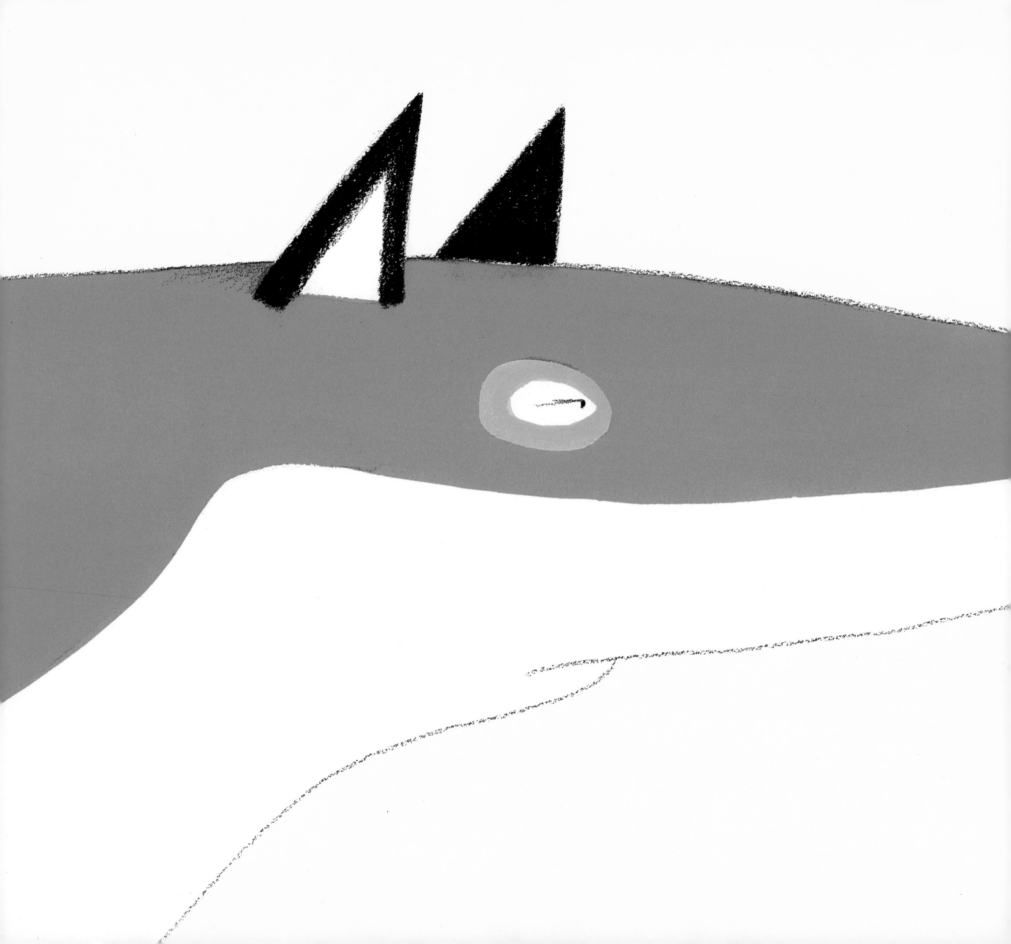

FOX!

EVERYBUNNY

Stay very still,
don't make a sound,
hold your breath
or you'll be found.

Everybunny
watch...

a dainty waltz,

a pirouette,

a somersault,

a clarinet,

a graceful bow,

a quiet sigh,

a lonely fox,

a tearful eye.

EVERYBUNNY CLAP!

And gather round,
and cheer and sing,
and call 'Bravo',
and all join in!

And run and jump,
and dance and play,

all together,

every day.

For Brian

MARGARET K. McELDERRY BOOKS
An imprint of Simon & Schuster Children's Publishing Division
1230 Avenue of the Americas, New York, New York 10020
Text and illustrations copyright © 2017 by Ellie Sandall
Originally published in Great Britain in 2017 by Hodder and Stoughton
Published by arrangement with Hodder and Stoughton Ltd.
All rights reserved, including the right of reproduction in whole or
in part in any form.
MARGARET K. McELDERRY BOOKS is a trademark of Simon &
Schuster, Inc.
For information about special discounts for bulk purchases, please contact
Simon & Schuster Special Sales at 1-866-506-1949 or
business@simonandschuster.com.
The Simon & Schuster Speakers Bureau can bring authors to your
live event. For more information or to book an event, contact the
Simon & Schuster Speakers Bureau at 1-866-248-3049 or visit our
website at www.simonspeakers.com.
Book design by Ann Bobco
The text for this book was set in P22Garamouche.
Manufactured in China
1016 HCB
First Edition
10 9 8 7 6 5 4 3 2 1
CIP data for this book is available from the Library of Congress.
ISBN 978-1-4814-9822-7
ISBN 978-1-4814-9823-4 (eBook)